TIG in the DUMPS

Written by Michaela Morgan
Illustrated by Mike Phillips

1 In Trouble

Tig always *tried* to sit still. Tig always *tried* not to wriggle. But he just *couldn't* stay still.

It seemed as if his head was full of dreams and his pants were full of ants. And the school chairs really were very hard.

"Have you heard a word I've said?" asked Miss Simmons.

"Oh yes, Miss!" said Tig. "I heard every word."
"Well, what did I say, then?"

Tig thought for a moment. "Can't you
remember, Miss?" he wondered.

Miss Simmons exploded. "Are you trying to be cheeky?"
"No, Miss!" Tig protested. "I'm not trying to be
cheeky at all."

It was true. Tig never *tried* to be cheeky. He never
tried to get into trouble. In fact, he always
tried to be good.

But somehow, things just never worked out.

He had heard every word Miss Simmons had said.
She'd said:

Tomorrow is Book Day.

You can all dress up as a book character.

There is a **fantastic** prize for the best costume.

And **please** think carefully about your costume.

Last year everybody came as pop singers. Try to be **different**!

"Think of all the lovely books you've read in school. Look!" Miss Simmons waved her hand at a display of books and posters. "You could be a character from any of these books. You could be ...

... a detective ...

... or a hobbit ...

... or a superhero."

2 Little Boy Blue

All that day, Miss Simmons went on about Book Day.
"You could dress up as a pirate. Or you could be my
favourite character, Stig of the Dump. You all enjoyed
Stig of the Dump when we read it, didn't you? It's about
a boy who finds a real Cave Boy in a pit, remember?'

Miss Simmons sounded determined.
"There are lots of characters you could be.
**I don't want to see you all dressed as pop stars
this Book Day**."

At playtime everyone decided which characters they were going to be.

Tig hoped nobody was going to remember the costume
he wore last year.

He didn't need anyone to remind him. How could he forget? His mum had gone to lots of trouble to make his costume. She always tried her best at things. She'd made him a tiger costume. But she'd made one tiny mistake.

Can you spot it?

How the tiger got its spots

Kev and Katy had been quick to notice the mistake.
They always picked on Tig.

Even Tig's friends gave him a hard time. All day long
they went on about it.

That's how he got his nickname, Tig.
But after a while, he started to like it.

Tig wanted to wear his football kit for the Book Day competition this year. He didn't want to look different again! But when he got home and told his mum, she had other ideas. She wanted him to wear something special.

Just look at it!

a straw hat

a frilly blue shirt

velvet trousers

a silky belt

shiny shoes

big shiny buckles

"Your aunty had this in the loft," said Mum.
"I promised we'd look after it really carefully.
It's a Little Boy Blue costume. I can make it fit you."

As she tugged and tweaked at the costume, she sang the song:

Little Boy Blue come blow on your horn.
The sheep's in the meadow,
The cow's in the corn.
But where is the boy who looks after the sheep?
He's under a haystack fast asleep!

Tig wished **he** was under a haystack.

He knew what Katy and Kev would do when they saw him in the costume. He could just imagine it ...

3 The Perfect Plan

That night, Tig had nightmares about
the Little Boy Blue suit. He couldn't stop worrying.
What could he do?

There were only three possible plans he could think of:

1 Pretend to be sick and stay off school.
2 Hide in the PE cupboard all day.
3 Run away.

Then Tig had a much better idea. It was perfect!
And at last he could fall asleep.

In the morning Tig put on his Little Boy Blue costume, picked up his sports bag, waved goodbye to Mum and set off. But he didn't go far.
He had his plan!

He crouched behind the hedge at the end of
next door's garden.

Then he took out his football kit.
Carefully, very carefully, he took off
the frilly blue shirt. He folded it to put it in his bag.

Have you guessed the plan?

Yes! Tig was going to wear his football kit as his costume for Book Day. Then he was going to change back into the Little Boy Blue costume just before he went home for tea with Mum.

That was his clever plan. Nobody would laugh at him and he wouldn't hurt Mum's feelings. Nothing could go wrong.

Or could it?

Tig had just put the last bit of the terrible blue costume into his sports bag when he heard a growl.

He looked around and what did he see? It was the dog from next door.

GRRRRR

GRRRRR

Tig was a bit scared of this dog. In fact, he was terrified of it. It had shiny, sharp teeth. It had slobbering jaws. It had feet as big as frying pans. And it had a very nasty look in its eye.

It was looking at him. Then – it snapped its jaws shut and came towards him.

Tig didn't wait to find out if the dog was feeling friendly. He was off and running for his life! Clutching his bag, he ran right through the hedge. Then through next door's compost heap ...

... through a garden pond ...

... over a strawberry patch ...

... through another hedge ...

... and then there he was ...

... in the school playground,
wearing only his underpants.

He was also wearing quite a lot of pond weed, some mud, bits of straw, twigs and some grass cuttings. This is what he looked like.

Could it get any worse?

4 "Phew!"

Yes, it could. He had been seen.

A group of people came towards Tig. They were staring at him and pointing. It was just like his nightmare!
He could see Katy and Kevin and his teacher,
Miss Simmons.

He was in trouble. Deep trouble.

First to speak was Kev.

"Phew!" he said.

But before he could carry on, Miss Simmons butted in.

"Yes!" she said. "You look just like Stig of the Dump. *Brilliant!* ***Fantastic! DIFFERENT!***"

All the other kids were footballers and princesses.
They stared at Tig.
Then one by one they said:

Even Kev looked impressed.

And of course ... Tig won the prize. It was
an enormous box of chocolates.
He took them home, had a bath, changed his clothes
and gave the box of chocolates to Mum.

She was pleased.

"You've looked after the costume so well! It looks as good as new!" she said. "Why, it almost looks as if it had never been worn."

Then she smiled and ate a chocolate.
"Nutty – but nice!" she laughed.
And she gave him a big hug.

Tig's Different Costumes

a straw hat

a frilly blue shirt

a silky belt

velvet trousers

big shiny buckles

shiny shoes

embarrassing costume

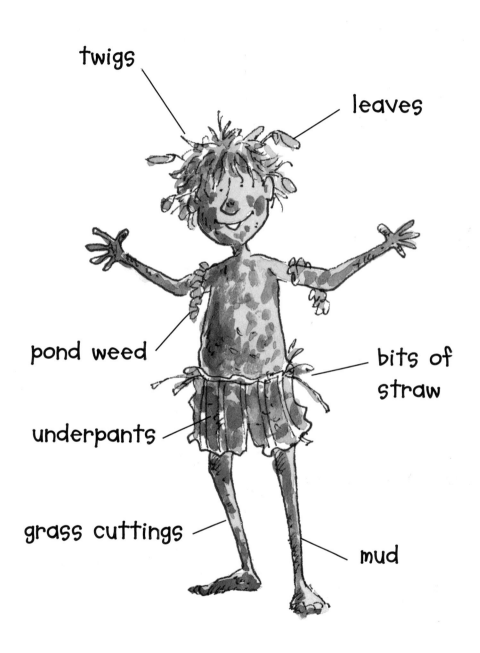

twigs

leaves

pond weed

bits of straw

underpants

grass cuttings

mud

prize—winning costume

Ideas for guided reading

Learning objectives: understand time and sequential relationships in stories, i.e. what happened when; identify and describe characters; express own views using words and phrases from texts; take account of grammar and punctuation, when reading aloud; speak with clarity and use intonation when reading and reciting texts.

Curriculum links: Citizenship: Choices and Taking Part

Interest words: protested, determined, velvet, tweaked, imagine, nightmares, crouched, slobbering, compost heap, impressed, enormous

Word count: 1,213

Resources: whiteboard and coloured pens

Getting started

This book can be read over two guided reading sessions.

- Read the title to the children, asking them what they think it means to be 'in the dumps'. They may have heard of the expression 'down in the dumps'. Does the title remind anybody of another book they may have heard of? (*Stig of the Dump* by Clive King.)

- Look together at the cover and illustrations from pp2–4. *What kind of character do you think Tig is?* Read to the group using expression to establish Tig's character.

- Ask the children to say what kind of character Miss Simmons is. How will her voice sound in the speech bubbles on p5? Ask a child to demonstrate. Discuss the use of bold and italic print for emphasis.

Reading and responding

- Ask the children to read the text quietly up to Chapter 3. Then ask them to predict what happens, based on their knowledge of Tig. *Will everything go to plan? What could go wrong?*

- Ask the children to continue reading independently, inviting each child in turn to read a short section aloud to you. Prompt and praise accurate reading. As they read, remind the children to observe punctuation and use expression to add character and meaning.

- When they reach the end, ask the children if 'Tig in the Dumps' is a good title for this story and why.